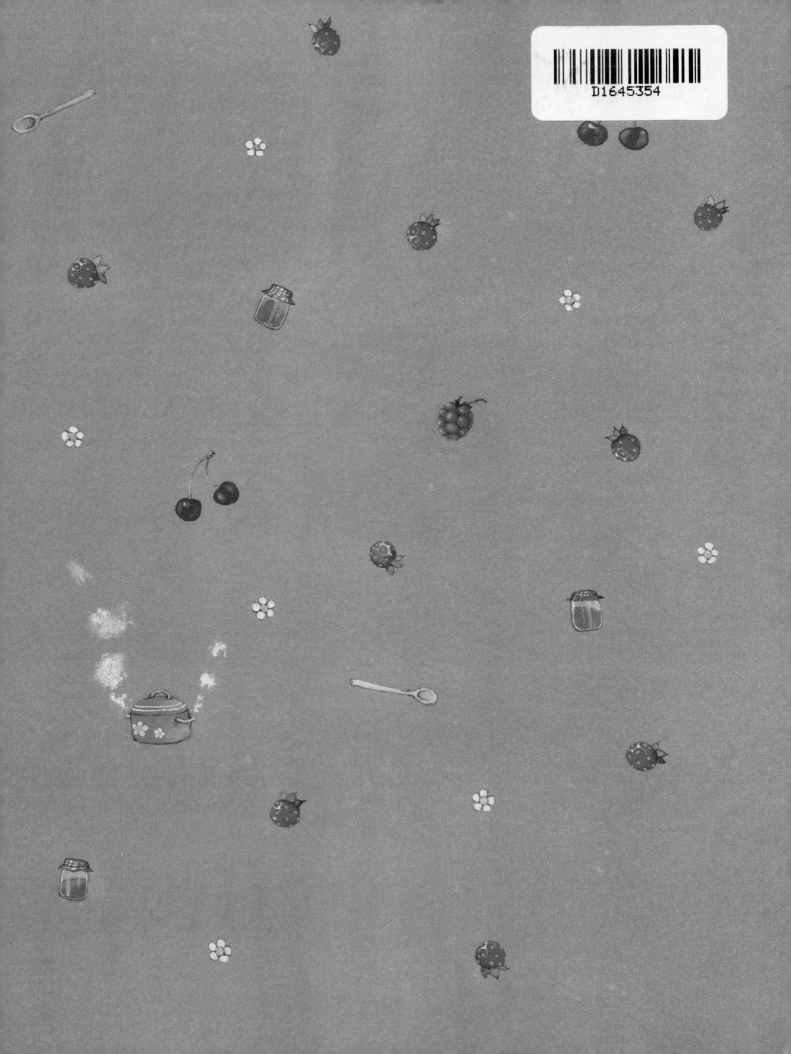

Brightwing Butterfly

Summer the Sunshine Fairy

Evie the Strawberry Fairy

Laurel the Tree Sprite

Hedgehog

The illustrations in this book are hand-drawn using pencils, watercolour paint, pastels and gouache.

Translated by Polly Lawson. First published in German as *Erdbeerinchen Erdbeerfee. Das Geheimnis im Beerenwald* by Arena Verlag GmbH 2015. First published in English by Floris Books in 2020 Story and illustrations by Stefanie Dahle. English version © 2020 Floris Books. All rights reserved. No part of this publication may be reproduced without the prior permission of Floris Books, Edinburgh www.florisbooks.co.uk British Library CIP data available ISBN 978-178250-638-6 Printed in Malaysia by Tien Wah Press

MIX
Paper from
responsible sources
FSC
www.fsc.org   FSC® C012700

Floris Books supports sustainable forest management by printing this book on materials made from wood that comes from responsible sources and reclaimed material

Evie the Strawberry Fairy

Evie and the Strawberry Surprise

Stefanie Dahle

Floris Books

Strange and surprising things were
happening in Wildberry Acres.
    First, Evie the Strawberry Fairy
couldn't find her magic wand.
She looked all around her
garden, even under the
flower pots.

"Have you seen it?" Evie asked her best friend
Brightwing Butterfly.

"Maybe you dropped it in Berry Woods yesterday,"
suggested Brightwing. "But never mind your wand,
come quickly and look at this!"

Evie ran across the garden and gasped. "Oh, what a
strawberry surprise – my berries have turned bright blue!"

Just then, the phone rang.

Evie picked it up: her friend hedgehog's
voice was full of worry.

"Come over right away!" she told him.

Soon afterwards, hedgehog arrived, huffing
and puffing. Evie's friends Summer the Sunshine
Fairy and Laurel the Tree Sprite fluttered in at the
same time. They all seemed troubled.

"Look, I'm splattered in red spots!" gasped hedgehog.
"My pale hair has turned bright orange!" blurted Laurel.
"And I've lost my happy sunshine feeling!" wailed Summer.

"And it's all because a scary Hogwotchit has moved into Berry Woods!" they shouted together.

Evie couldn't help giggling. "A Hogwotchit? What's a Hogwotchit? It doesn't sound very scary."

"The Hogwotchit is huge!" Summer exclaimed. "I only saw its shadow, but I've felt frightened ever since."

"It has magical powers!" Laurel cried. "It changed the colour of my hair!"

"It's mean," hedgehog growled. "It gave me these horrible spots!"

"And it's also VERY LOUD!" they all said at once.

Evie sighed. "If only I had my magic wand, I could fix you all," she said.

"Maybe you didn't lose your wand, Evie," hedgehog said. "Maybe the Hogwotchit has stolen it! That's how he's doing all this magic."

Evie wasn't sure. She didn't know anything about the Hogwotchit. But then again, *someone* had turned her strawberries blue...

"Let's hunt for this Hogwotchit and find out," she decided. "I'll pack my bag."

Evie and Brightwing Butterfly hurried
inside to look for anything that might help
them deal with a Hogwotchit.
Evie rummaged in her big chest.
She pondered seed pods and plant pots,
feathers that tickle and jars of old pickle.

"Let's go, Evie," called hedgehog, Summer and Laurel.
"Coming!" She quickly bundled some gardening wire,
a small trowel and an enchanted pink raincloud into a bag.

The friends crept cautiously into Berry Woods.
Soon they heard loud thumps and crashes.
   "That's where the Hogwotchit lives,"
whispered Summer, pointing ahead.
   Then hedgehog stopped so suddenly that
Evie stumbled into his spines!
   "Ouch! What is it?" she asked.
   "It must be the H-H-H-Hogwotchit!"
cried Summer, Laurel and hedgehog.

Evie looked. A small furry animal was standing
beneath a broken tin-can house.
"Is that really the Hogwotchit? It's so small," she said.
"It's just a little vole!" added Brightwing.

The Hogwotchit turned around and cried, "Excuse me, I am not *just* a vole. I am the berry best jam-maker in Wildberry Acres!"

Suddenly, there was a loud **BANG!** Steam billowed and sticky red droplets flew through the air. Everyone gasped – including the vole.

"Do you need some help?" asked Evie kindly.

Vole hung his head. "I had summer fruit left over, so I was making jam for winter. But it keeps going horribly wrong!"

"Hmm. Let's see," said Evie, flying cautiously
closer to vole's open door.

"I think it might be the new spoon I found," vole continued.
"Ever since I started stirring with it, my jam has been
misbehaving."

Inside, among the splodges of sticky, jammy mess, Evie spotted something familiar. "Hey, that's not a spoon... That's my magic wand! And it's broken!" she cried.

Vole looked embarrassed. "I'm very sorry, I didn't know."

He reached for the wand when suddenly it bounced up and whizzed about, knocking into everything. It would have crashed into Brightwing, but hedgehog stuck out his foot and trapped it, just in time.

"The stove is on fire!" shouted Evie. "My broken wand
can't put it out!" Then she remembered the enchanted cloud
she had packed. "Rain, little cloud!"

The cloud pitter-pattered on the flames until they
went out with a hiss.

Vole looked sadly at the mess. "How will I stir my jam now?"

Evie remembered something else in her bag.

"You could try this little trowel," she suggested.
Vole took it happily.

Evie turned to her friends. "There *is* no Hogwotchit! It was only vole's exploding jam dripping red spots on hedgehog and turning Laurel's hair orange. I think my strawberries probably turned blue when the wand broke."

Summer realised that there was nothing to be scared of. She beamed with happiness.

Together, they all washed hedgehog and Laurel, and then helped vole clean his house. Evie used her gardening wire to repair the broken shelves.

Later, the new friends celebrated with a picnic, including vole's delicious jam cookies!

Evie smiled. Her wand was mended,
and everyone was happy.

"Remember you still need to fix your blue
strawberries when we get home," said Brightwing.

"Perhaps I'll leave a few blue and give them
to vole," giggled Evie. "Blue strawberry jam really
would be a surprise!"

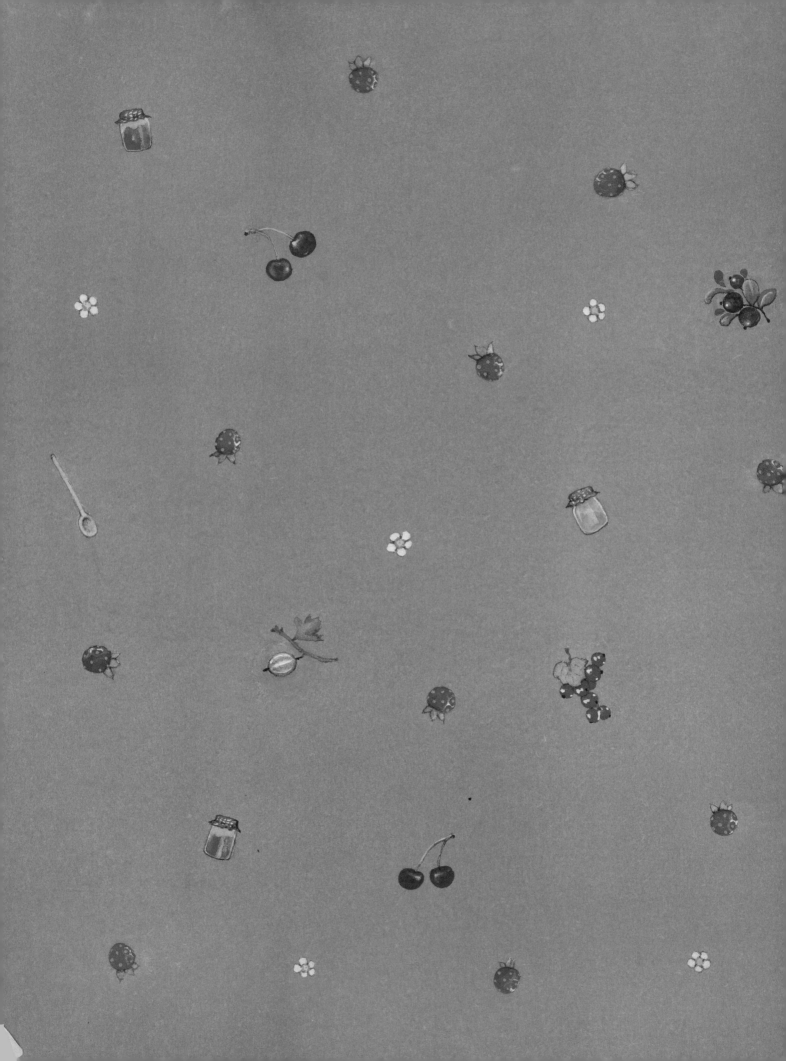